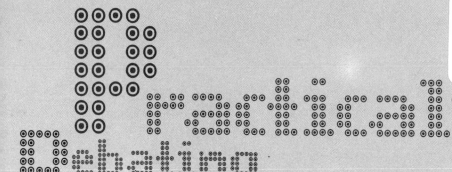

实用辩论技巧

Sue Kay（英）著

a simple guide to the art of debate in English

外语教学与研究出版社
FOREIGN LANGUAGE TEACHING AND RESEARCH PRESS
北京　BEIJING

图书在版编目(CIP)数据

实用辩论技巧 = Practical Debating：a simple guide to the art of debate in English ／（英）凯
（Kay，S.）著 .— 北京：外语教学与研究出版社，2006.4
ISBN 7－5600－5440－4

Ⅰ. 实… Ⅱ. 凯… Ⅲ. 英语—辩论—自学参考资料—英文 Ⅳ. H311. 9

中国版本图书馆 CIP 数据核字 (2006) 第 023621 号

出 版 人：李朋义
责任编辑：张晓芳
封面设计：刘 冬
出版发行：外语教学与研究出版社
社 址：北京市西三环北路 19 号 (100089)
网 址：http：//www.fltrp.com
印 刷：北京大学印刷厂
开 本：787×1092 1/16
印 张：7.25
版 次：2006 年 4 月第 1 版 2006 年 4 月第 1 次印刷
书 号：ISBN 7－5600－5440－4
定 价：12.90 元
＊ ＊ ＊

ACKNOWLEDGEMENTS

It is impossible to credit everyone who deserves credit for the information in this handbook. My passion for debate was sparked when I attended the University of Glasgow Union Debates in my youth and my interest has continued throughout life.

I am indebted to the organisers of the FLTRP Cup National English Debating Competition for their support and interest and for clarifying a number of issues about debate in China.

I am also indebted to Loke Wing Fatt and his team from the Society for Associated Inter-Tertiary Debaters (SAID) in Singapore. Their lectures and training have been very helpful as well as entertaining — as all good debates should be!

Finally, my gratitude to all the debaters who have had the courage to stand up and debate in public. They have pioneered the way and we have all learnt from their efforts.

Contents

Introduction

L earning any language requires more than acquiring the ability to correctly use grammar and vocabulary. Understanding how a language is used and the cultural mores that underpin its use is essential. That is why I think it is so important that English language learners learn how to debate in English. Debating in English demands ability to reason and substantiate, to structure and develop arguments and to interpret and argue from opposing viewpoints. These skills will prove invaluable when using English.

This short handbook aims to help readers to start on the road to acquiring the art of debate. Not everyone will become world-class debaters but the journey will broaden perspectives, highlight current issues and at the same time help understanding of how the English language can be used.

People who use this book want to learn how to debate or have an interest in its role in language. It should be clear that debate is not only confined to university competitive debates but that once mastered, it will be useful in business and social forums throughout life.

I have put most of the technical information about how to debate into 3 parts: Manner, Method, Matter. However, this is merely a useful way to separate all the elements of a formal debate. It should be remembered that the techniques can be used in many different ways and that these may not all be formal nor competitive.

PART 1

The Why and What of Debate

Debate is fundamental to the use of the English language. Not being able to debate is one of the reasons why people who have mastered the grammar and vocabulary of English find it difficult to make their voices heard when mixing with native speakers. Therefore, learning how to debate is extremely useful for all English learners.

Not everyone can debate in public. It takes courage, quick thinking and flexibility. However, debate provides knowledge, best solutions, clarity and speed of thought, self-confidence, friends and fun. Therefore, it is worth understanding even if you have no intention of taking part in competitions. Be warned though, once mastered, it is addictive and you are likely to find that you seek out fellow debaters wherever you are.

Before explaining how to debate, it is useful to know why people debate and what it is.

Why Debate?

In China, students are intrigued, incredulous and even shocked when

I tell them that one of the first words a western child learns to use is "why". It is not part of the Asian tradition to question the reasons and motives of one's elders and betters — but this is not the case in the West.

To take this a step further, in the West, both parent and child know that if the question "why?" is answered with "because I said so" there has been failure. Western culture demands that assertions are substantiated — that reasons are given for statements. It is this reasoning that underpins much of the practical use of English as well as other European languages, both written and spoken.

In this globalising world, debate is an essential skill because debate will not only reinforce information and so increase knowledge, it will expand understanding about how information can be used, extended and broadened. Furthermore, in most societies it is understood that debate in the form of discussion makes us realize that we are not alone with our problems — that our problems are not unique and that we can learn much from each other if we share our ideas and experiences — a two way sharing!

People discuss or debate, that is, share views, engage in mutual and reciprocal critique in order to:

- help understanding

- enhance self-awareness and ability and ideas

- foster tolerance and appreciation of opposing views

- provide a forum for informed decision making

The modern world of business is one of strategic decision making. As such, it requires a great deal of flexibility in thinking and breadth of understanding (which is often achieved by taking into consideration many different opinions) as well as specialist knowledge.

Many Chinese business people, with considerable knowledge in their fields and with excellent command of English language, find it hard to make their voices heard. At meetings with their international counterparts, they are disadvantaged and even marginalized by not understanding the need to — or how to — debate issues. Challenge is not considered rude in western society so long as it is appropriately done.

Generally, business people find they have to have ability to:

- converse socially and professionally in an open and constructive way

- take a constructive part in meetings

- formulate their own opinion and argue it at all levels, i.e. with peers, superiors and juniors

- be able to defend decisions

- challenge existing and proposed policies

- propose options

Benefits of Debate

- Training in debate improves analytical skills because all assertions have to be substantiated.

- Debate improves speaking skills because persuasion means you have to think about how best to say something and how to clarify your ideas.

- Debate will ensure that data is evaluated before it can be used to support an argument, otherwise the data and the idea it supports may be challenged.

- Training in debate means that previously held information will be assessed for reliability.

- Debate contributes to the intellectual development of people and of society by ensuring that alternative perspectives are considered.

- Debate helps to deepen understanding and widen knowledge.

• Debate improves critical thinking and can change or modify attitudes.

• Debate develops awareness and respect for others' opinions and by doing so helps develop social communication skills.

• Debate improves self-confidence and speaking ability through having to agree, disagree, question, ask for clarification, explain, interrupt, give opinion, sum up, or acting as chairperson (the Speaker).

• Debate highlights the importance of preparation.

• Taking part in a debate also has the surprising benefit of learning that it is alright to fail. If you lose a debate, you have still performed a valuable service because you will have highlighted inconsistencies and tested the reliability of the opposition's arguments.

Results from Debating

• Debate helps create new ideas and solutions — which of course are essential to survival in a competitive world.

• It helps to solve problems in the best possible way and come to best decisions, both of which are so necessary in the business world.

• It ensures that assertions are sensibly substantiated and therefore that ideas, data, statistics and judgements are reasonable.

• It ensures that all voices are heard, i.e. all relevant knowledge tapped.

What Is Debate?

History of Debate

"The unexamined life is not worth living."

— Socrates

To most westerners debate began in the 5th C BC in Greece with the famous dialectics of Socrates, Plato and Aristotle.

Socrates was a sceptic — a good thing to be if you want to be able to debate — though, sadly, his sceptical views led to his early death. However, his methods and ideas have lived on through his pupils, through Roman law, theological debates and into systems of governance. He is generally judged to have been a highly intelligent person — still considered by many in the West to have been one of the wisest people ever to have lived.

Socrates taught the value of self-analysis through a method of cross questioning that challenged conventional wisdom. By doing so, it can be argued that he opened the door to change and progress. This is because <u>when an idea, policy, solution, argument or method is challenged, the strengths as well as the weaknesses become clearer</u>. The strengths can then be retained and even copied, whilst the weaknesses can be removed or changed. Another way to think about this is that by identifying the holes in an argument, the argument becomes clearer. It may be that there are so many holes that the idea is shown to be invalid, or perhaps some of the holes can be filled so that the argument becomes stronger.

Debate Today

Most people are probably unaware that nowadays Socrates' methods and ideas appear in many aspects of daily life. For example:

- the daily meetings that constitute business practice
- in the education and upbringing of children
- in universities and research institutions where existing knowledge is explored and challenged in order to be increased
- in social conversation at all levels

Debate therefore underpins much of the use of the English language so understanding what it is will help language learners to use English more effectively.

Definitions

Dialectic is the investigation of the truth of opinions especially by logical discussion. It comes from the Greek words *dialektike tekhne* meaning "art of debate".

Dialectics are logical discussions which investigate the truth of opinions that challenge and question conventional wisdom (that is, normally accepted practices and thinking). These logical discussions make us search for greater understanding of the world around us and think about and look for better solutions to the problems we encounter.

Example:

> *When water is scarce, why do people still clean their teeth under a running tap?*
>
> *Being challenged, they may well decide that they can change their habit and use a tumbler or cup instead. This might save a lot of water every year especially in urban areas.*

Discussion can be thought of as debate — indeed many conversations are debate. During conversation, people often explore ideas and possibilities, challenge existing ideas and exchange reasons in order to better understand the world around them.

However, discussion is often formalised so that order and rules can be applied. This happens in business meetings when the chairman of the meeting will impose order and set an agenda and in many other forums when it may be called debate.

Debate is defined as "an exchange of reasoning". In other words, it is a questioning exploration that is changing, energetic and dynamic. Debate depends on there being opposing or at least alternative views since it is impossible to have a debate if everyone agrees or appears to agree. It is the exchange and exploration of views during debate that will allow the participants and listeners to increase their knowledge and understanding, to develop their ideas and to create new ideas.

Formal debate is held under clearly defined rules which maintain order and provide structure; allow the speakers to fulfill their roles in a fair manner; allocate time and provide clear criteria for assessment. They take place in many universities and institutions throughout the world.

Competitive debating is formal debating in which winning is important. Whilst the exchange of reasoning continues there is an added element of <u>persuasion in order to win</u>. This requires clear and logical analysis of issues and a decision about which arguments to adopt. The aim is to:

1. convince the audience — and judges — that your argument has the greater strength

2. show that your analysis of the problem is valid and thorough

3. show how the change (see Part 2) you propose is worthy despite the challenges offered by the opposition

4. be persuasive through clear reasoning and use of persuasive language

A good competitive debater is attempting to win the exchange by having stronger arguments and also by showing the opposition's arguments to be weaker and therefore of less importance. The debater does this by analyzing the subject and by well reasoned critical analysis of the opposition's arguments.

Competitive debating at universities allows for many and varied topics to be explored.

Example:

> *Motion—"Formal Examinations Are the Best Assessment of Ability."*

PRO — *Examination success indicates:*	CON — *Poor ability may indicate:*
Good memory	Inability to control nerves in some situations
Good understanding	An "off" day
Good control of nerves	Lack of knowledge or understanding which may be acquired later when it is relevant
Ability to think quickly	Slow thinking but maybe deeper thinking

The purpose of the motion is to assess the strength and weakness of examinations as being the best way to assess ability. This follows from the implication or premise that passing examinations fits people for better or more responsible jobs.

In the list above, you can see that there are opposing views. These are <u>explored through analysis and reasoning</u> during the debate. The argument about nerves, for example, aims to come to a conclusion as to whether being able to control nerves in an examination will indicate an ability that is useful in life.

Example:

The reasoning about nerves might explore:

is it necessary to control nerves? ■ *relevance to working life* ■ *the need for a variety of skills* ■ *not all skilled jobs require strong nerves* ■ *advantage / disadvantage of confidence in the workplace* ■ *methods of controlling nerves* ■ *the advantages / disadvantages of adrenalin in the body when under pressure* ■ *ability to think clearly when under pressure* ■ *the use of pressure as a motivating force.*

An **argument** can be a fight or a quarrel (an unpleasant, usually rather childish experience), but it can also mean <u>a set of reasons given in support</u> of something in order to persuade. Argument is the process of explaining <u>why</u> a point of view should be accepted. <u>An argument is not an assertion.</u> It includes the <u>logic and the evidence supporting</u> a particular claim or conclusion.

In order for an argument to be persuasive, it may be necessary to provide more than one reason to support an assertion or claim. A number of reasons, all with examples and /or statistics will be more difficult to disagree with than one. Also, if the reason given is complex or ambiguous, it may be important, in order to persuade, to provide reasons for the reason!

Example:

"*Capital punishment should be banned.*"

One reason may be that it fails to prevent or reduce crime because criminals are not rational: 1) they don't expect to be caught, crime has only any logic if criminals don't expect to be caught; 2) many crimes are not planned, for example, crimes of passion are generally impetuous rather than planned (in order to make this reason more persuasive you could tell a short story of love and passion leading to crime to prove the point); 3) someone who is in the grip of great emotion such as hate, fear or panic is unable to act rationally because they are unable to think straight, (again provide an example of a relevant case to make your reasoning clear and persuasive and/or some medical evidence to prove the point).

— *Making an argument therefore has 3 elements:* —

1. it entails making a point   S   statement

2. giving the reason for that point   EX   explanation

3. supplying evidence to back up the reasons   I   illustration

— A GOOD DEBATER IS THEREFORE SEXI! —

Note We can see that in debate it is the train of reasoning that is important not the conclusion. We may not like or personally agree with the conclusion that our reasoning brings us to, but if the reasoning is logical and follows from the premise then it will be a good argument.

A **premise** is an underlying assumption, that is, the statement from which other statements can be inferred.

Example:
_____

"*Smoking is bad for health*" *follows from an underlying premise that people can affect their health by how they behave.*

Example:
_____

"*Education is a basic right of all children*" *follows from an underlying premise that children can have rights and also, from perhaps an unfounded premise, that education is or can be available wherever there are children.*

Note Debate differs from making a speech because in debate written speeches are not permitted. This prevents the reading out of long boring statements. The argument must be extemporaneous, that is, spoken without preparation (at least without obvious preparation) so that the <u>speakers respond to and challenge</u> what the other side says — that is, they can not just state their opinion whilst ignoring opposing ideas and arguments and expect to be believed.

Styles of Debate

There are many different styles of debate:

1. Some, as I have mentioned above, are informal such as a **discussion**.Discussion may be just conversation or conversation that is regulated with rules and procedures which may be different in different circumstances. For example, in a business context, the discussion will be organised, probably by a chairman, so that decisions can be made or policy formed.

2. There is **cross examination** where a person puts his point of view and is then questioned by two or more separate adversaries — this is common in many courts of law.

3. Even **public speaking** can be a form of debate as we saw in the so-called "presidential debates" in America. Care must be taken with this: <u>a debate is not just a speech</u>.

4. **Free argumentation** is another form of debate but it can be problematic. Unless speakers are given sufficient time to develop their points, the lack of depth in the arguments means

that the debate often degenerates into a quarrel.

5. **Parliamentary style debating** (sometimes called dialectic style debating) is the most common form of academic debate in universities the world over because it encourages and requires the clash, in other words, the challenge. This is the heart of debate and although the rules may differ in different countries or institutions, the substance will be the same. Debate is about disagreement and winning, no matter the costs. For example, you may have to argue a point of view that you personally disagree with in order to win the argument. In other words, you may have to "play devils advocate".

▶ The form or style of parliamentary debating is flexible and is set and followed in different ways in different countries. There are differences in the number of teams on each side, in the number of people in each team, in the preparation and speaking times allowed, in the names given to the sides competing and in the roles appropriate to each speaker as well as the rules about rebuttals, motions and definitions.

For example, the **standard American style** has two teams of two contestants making a total of 6 speeches because one speaker will speak twice by giving a "reply" speech.

The **standard British style** brings a greater level of complexity by having four competing teams, two teams on each side each comprising of two people making a total of 8 speeches. Each team has a specific role to play depending on their order of speaking. For example, the summing up for the whole side is done by the last speakers of the second teams.

Even judging is different.

Adjudication in the UK

In the UK, judges can bring a reasonable level of knowledge to their assessment of the debate contents so that in theory it is possible for teams to win by providing the best argument. If a judge knows that a side has made an incorrect statement he can mark down for that. Marks will be given for strong arguments, effective rebuttals and speakers who fulfill their roles correctly.

Adjudication in the US

In the USA, judges have to be told everything within the debate. For example, if a debater says that Canada should join NATO, it is up to the opposing side to say that Canada is already a member; otherwise, the judge must give the point to the first side, if it is a relevant argument, even though it is incorrect. This can mean

> that in America the affirmative side will usually win unless the negative side destroys every point of its argument.
>
> The British style is most common at the World Championships, except when it takes place in America.

Uses of Debate

Debate in Education

In education, debate allows participants to reinforce their knowledge by explaining and defending. By doing so, they are able to clarify their ideas and to develop their ability to reason effectively since ideas that are not logical or relevant will be "attacked". It is therefore a useful teaching methodology.

Debate at Work

At work, debate offers opportunities to resolve issues by achieving the "best" solution in the circumstances. Business meetings are often a forum to debate a problem or policy in order to identify best solutions or systems. Debate helps to identify weak solutions and policies and to strengthen possible options.

Debate for Life

Be aware that formal competitive debating is training for life. Just as a university student may never write another essay, they may never take part in another debating competition outside of their university. However, the logical and analytical method of thinking will be very valuable for the rest of their lives.

CONCLUSION

 Training in debate improves analytical skills and speaking skills. Having done so, people are then able to defend their judgements and their judgements will be more effective.

 Debate is defined as an exchange of argument and an argument is a set of reasons given in support of a view in order to persuade — especially in formal debates, arguments must be challenged!

 Because of the variety of styles and rules, it is important that whenever asked to debate, you need to first ask about the rules and criteria under which the debate will take place. Remember though that although the rules and criteria may vary, the basics of debate are much the same.

PART 2

Preparation

I think that to a degree good debaters are born not made. There are people in this world who really don't care about the big issues, who, for example, prefer to understand their surroundings through music or art or who are quick to agree with whatever is said so long as they don't have to make a decision, give an opinion or do anything. Fortunately there are many others who are naturally curious or argumentative, who question everything and everyone and who are interested in what is going on, how the world turns and who is making it turn. Such people are likely to make good debaters.

Preparing for Debate

We may not all become great debaters but we can all prepare for debate and learn the techniques of how to become effective debaters. Preparation can be done in many different and interesting ways.

1. Be aware of current affairs. For example, watch both the international and domestic news everyday. Read newspapers and magazines which comment on the news.

2. Think about the reasons why people, agencies and governments do what they do and develop your own ideas about what effects the actions may have.

3. Try to identify the issues of the day and analyse them from as many different perspectives as possible, not only from your own point of view or experience.

4. Increase your fund of knowledge. For example, the countries which belong to ASEAN, what ASEAN stands for; the average GDP per capita of developed, developing and underdeveloped countries; the main medical hazards to health of smoking, drinking, taking drugs; a few basic statistics relating to major issues such as pollution; learn a few famous quotations and how to use them.

5. Understand that issues such as the death penalty, euthanasia and abortion are debated around the world and that there are no easy "right" or "correct" answers.

6. Be aware that the "biggies" such as modernization, development, human rights, environmentalism, gender, all have many varied and complex sub-issues that can be debated individually or within the larger context.

7. Identify a number of points or arguments to support or oppose ideas. Then research so that you are able to provide some statistics and examples to help persuade the audience to your side. Just making an assertion will not persuade.(see Part 5)

Preparation for debate goes on all the time (as does debate) by thinking about the big issues and trying to list the pros and cons of attitudes, solutions and policies so that you have clear ideas in your mind when you tackle a motion at short notice or if the affirmative side in a competition comes up with an obscure definition. "Knowing stuff", keeping up with the news, looking beyond the obvious and remembering main points, occasional statistics and short quotations will be helpful.

Example:

Analysing "Modernisation" — it can be argued "for"(generally equated to industrialization which allows people to leave farming and earn money; improved living conditions, for example, greater choice in shops and life style; development of technology which improves standards of living, for example, medicine, agricultural production...) or "against" (destruction of traditions, for example, the development of a global village which reduces variety; higher costs which the poor can't meet; urbanization which separates us from nature; pollution ...)

Therefore, debaters should prepare by:

1. making judgements or having opinions that they can defend with effective reasoning

2. critically looking into complex issues in order to analyse them for themselves

3. questioning commonly held beliefs

4. evaluating statistics, data and information as to whether they are reasonable

5. becoming aware of and considering alternative points, solutions or ideas

This last point is important. In order to prepare for debate you have to think of as many different points of view as you can about any topic. Once you have identified a point of view, then think about the arguments and importantly the counter arguments. Ask yourself, why do intelligent people disagree? Then think about the evidence that supports the arguments and counter arguments.

Example:

Topic — Age Discrimination

"This House believes that age discrimination should be made illegal in the workplace".

PROS	CONS
The elderly may be just as capable as the young	Old people may lose abilities, e.g. concentration and strength
The elderly have skills and experience	Hiring of labour should be based on ability
It goes against the idea of equality to prevent old people from working if they want to	A larger supply of workers may mean lower wages
More elderly workers means a bigger pool of skills and more competition	Employers will have to continue paying into pension schemes
The economy suffers because productivity is lower than it could be	Lack of promotion opportunities for younger people
Elderly people continuing to work reduces welfare and pension costs	Benefit costs get transferred to employers
Increases tax revenue	No evidence that a lack of mandatory retirement age means more elderly workers employed in Australia which has no compulsory retirement age

Motions

There are a number of different words to describe motions. They can be called, for example: topics, subjects, resolutions, moots, proposals, propositions or issues. Motions are usually worded as —

This House believes that ...

The **House** being the group of people taking part in <u>and</u> watching the debate. The affirmative side proposes the motion and the negative side opposes it. The audience is expected to watch and listen critically. They assess the persuasiveness of the arguments and come to a conclusion as to which argument is the strongest and whether the affirmative side has proved their case.

Motions generally are related to the current affairs, cultural mores and hot topics of the day. A look at any university debating club's website will give an indication of the current thinking and concerns in that region as well as providing ideas of commonly debated topics. There are thousands of possible motions but fewer subjects or issues since many motions relate to the same issues.

Common Motions — Topics of Debate

This House believes that beauty is skin-deep.

This House believes that cigarette advertising should be banned.

This House believes that crime does pay.

This House believes that corruption brings its own punishment.

This House believes that euthanasia should be legalized.

This House believes that housewives should be paid for their work.

This House believes that newspapers abuse their power.

This House believes that nuclear power is our best hope.

This House believes that one tree is worth a million rolls of newsprint.

This House believes that television has a destructive influence.

This House believes that the car is a curse.

Sometimes motions are rather philosophical and therefore may appear somewhat obtuse. It is important here to identify what the motion is addressing. This will usually be something of topical interest.

This House believes that a woman needs a man like a fish needs a bicycle. (feminism)

This House believes that experience is the best teacher. (nature versus nurture)

This House believes that green is an unhealthy colour. (environmentalism)

This House believes that life is too hectic to be happy. (modernization)

This House believes that reward is the best stimulus. (motivation)

This House believes that royalty is offensive. (monarchy versus republicanism)

This House believes that television is the new moral guardian. (influence of TV)

Purpose of the Motion

In parliamentary style debating, the motion identifies a problem or situation that could be changed. The purpose of the debate is to test whether the proposed change offered by the affirmative side in their definition of the motion is workable and reasonable.

Many debates are held to determine policy. It is worth thinking of this when you are faced with a motion. What is the problem being addressed by the motion? What policies could the affirmative side suggest to change the situation for the better? What effect — positive and negative — would they have if adopted? The negative side's burden (responsibility) is to test the proposal by challenging it with well thought out analytical reasoning. By doing so, the proposed policy is shown to be strong or weak.

Types of Motion

Subjects for debate can be straightforward or linked.

A **straightforward motion** provides a clear topic for the debate which will not be able to be interpreted in different ways.

Example:

> *"This house believes that college students should be allowed to cohabit." The underlying premise being that generally in China they are not allowed to cohabit but that some do and others would like to be able to. The subject of the debate is clear and requires little definition other than to perhaps narrow the definition of college students to a particular age group or level.*

Be careful not to redefine a straight motion.

Example:

> *If the motion is "This house would ban smoking cigarettes in public places", then that is what must be debated. There is only some room to define "public places" (enclosed places such as buildings or parks, streets etc.). (see Parts 4 and 5)*

Often straightforward motions are based on value comparisons which can be abstract rather than practical. They require a clash of philosophical values which test different ways of thinking about the motion and any underlying premise.

Example:

> *"This house despises flattery more than slander" or "This house*

believes that the local is preferable to the global."

A **linked motion** provides a topic that may be open to various interpretations. It is important that the interpretation chosen does show a clear link to the wording of the motion. The decision about how to interpret the subject may be influenced by what is currently in the news or currently under discussion among your peers.

Example:

"This house believes that vinyl records are better than compact discs."

This is an indication of a wider debate around popular disputes within the traditional versus modern debate. The definition can expand in many different ways and does not necessarily have to be about the music industry.

Example:

A motion "This house would not smoke" could, clearly, be about smoking, though it would also be possible to define the motion in terms of smoking chimneys and make it a debate about air pollution and the burning of fossil fuels. Again, the decision about how to define the motion may be influenced by what is currently in the news.

So, as we see, it is also possible to be given a motion that need not be debated literally and this leaves a lot of room for the affirmative side to set the limits of the debate through the definition.

Example:

"This house believes that it is better to die on one's feet than to live on one's knees."

There can be many different and equally valid interpretations of this. However, many can be related back to the big issues — in this case, perhaps "social responsibility": standing up for what you believe rather than going for the quiet life; having a go even if you are likely to fail rather than allowing nerves or laziness to control you; "better to have loved and lost than never to have loved at all". Another interpretation would be to do with "freedom": being prepared to fight rather than submit to unfair or excessive authority.

Defining a Motion

The affirmative side should remember that they have a duty (their burden) to provide a definition that will allow the negative side to debate. They should not try to cheat the negative side by defining a motion in obscure terms. (see Parts 4 and 5)

If the negative side is caught off guard by an unusual definition, they can complain by arguing that it is unreasonable. But unless it is clearly unreasonable (this is a subjective assessment that may not be agreed by the judges), they should agree to debate the definition given by the affirmative. The negative side's best strategy is to look at the wider context and use the more general arguments that they should know to argue against the given definition. Therefore being aware of the issues of the day is an important aspect of preparing for debate.

In competition, where there is usually a choice of 3 motions, the affirmative side can help themselves by choosing the motion that allows for the widest interpretation. This may allow them to surprise the negative side. The negative side should choose the motion (if they have a choice) that has the narrowest interpretation so that there is less chance of being surprised.

CONCLUSION

Preparation for debate goes on all the time. A useful strategy is to:

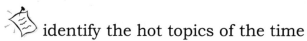 identify the hot topics of the time

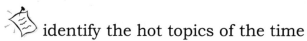 think about why intelligent people disagree about them

analyse the arguments for and against by working out the reasoning for the various views people may have

 identify examples to illustrate the reasons

 think about how the issues may be disguised in a motion

When faced with a motion:

 identify the underlying premise, problem or situation

 decide what will improve the situation — how, in what way?

 think about the pros and cons of the improvements. In other words, what are the arguments for and against?

PART 3

Manner

In competitive debating the judges have 3 main areas of focus:

Manner — delivery — how you speak and behave

Method — strategy — who does what, teamwork and analysis

Matter — content — the definition, arguments, evidence and rebuttals

Manner: how you say it

This is the key to success. It has been proved that 75% of communication is visual and only 25% verbal. Think how much more understandable anything is if you can see it rather than just hear it. Why has TV overtaken radio, why do we like to see our parents/children instead of just talking on the phone, why can we remember a word or number better if we have seen it written down?

Since the "how" is so important, it is worth looking at it in detail and also thinking about it when preparing for a debate.

Manner is the delivery style a debater uses to persuade the audience.

There are both physical and vocal aspects.

Physical Aspects of Manner

1. **Appearances** matter so dress appropriately

   • For a formal debate dress smartly — although student life is quite casual, generally people have a greater air of authority if they are smartly dressed.

2. Think about your **stance**

   • Don't stand like a guard on duty — it will make you tense and nervous and you'll look like a machine (who would believe an automaton?) — <u>Move</u>!

   • Lean forward, rest an elbow on the lectern sometimes — anything that seems natural to you and which helps to make your message clear. Be aware of the microphone though.

   • Finish on a strong note and stay still for it to sink in before you leave the platform.

   • Never turn your back on the audience.

3. **Gestures** should be natural

   • Gestures are necessary to add emphasis and to persuade.

   • Hold notes, if necessary, in one hand to leave your other hand free to gesture.

- Gestures must <u>not be repetitive</u> — practice in front of a mirror at home or, if you can, get someone to video you as you speak. That will allow you to see what works and what doesn't.

- If there is a high lectern in front of you, make sure hand gestures are visible above it.

- Use arms, hands and fingers to add emphasis.

- Use facial expression — frown, smile, shake your head or nod, raise an eyebrow (if you can) to show cynicism/skepticism. This can be done even when the opposition or your team member is speaking. It will help you to stay engaged and to show that you <u>are</u> engaged even though you are not speaking.

4. **Eye contact** has an enormous effect

- Make eye contact with all parts of the audience not just with the judges or a few people in the front row.

- If you wear glasses, don't hide behind a glass wall! They can be a great prop if sometimes you remove them (if you are long sighted) or peer over the top of the rim.

- Looking directly into people's eyes has a very persuasive effect.

5. **Style** — be yourself but plan for variety

- Individuals have their own style and it would be a mistake to try to change it. However, you may be able to improve it by working on it and looking for role models.

- There is no correct style. The best style is the one that helps you win! It is not helpful to tell your audience that you are feeling nervous or that you find the topic difficult. You may get a sympathetic reaction, but you won't have helped your argument.

- Try to discover which aspects of your style are the best for communication and are the most persuasive.

- Can you adapt your style convincingly to the situation? For example, you may at different points in the debate need to decide whether you want to appear: rational or passionate; calm or aggressive; serious or humourous.

Your decision will depend on the subject, on how you intend to tackle the subject and on how the opposition behaves. If they use a loud, passionate delivery then you may be better to adopt a calm rational approach rather than trying to out-yell them. On the other hand, if the opposition is calm and rational, or the debate has become a bit stuck, a more passionate or humorous delivery will add some sparkle and may earn you some support.

6. Use of **notes**

- <u>Notes must not be a distraction</u>. Constantly waving, fluttering or crackling paper eventually will cause the audience to think about the notes not about what you are saying.

- <u>Don't read</u>. You must not read your speech. That is, you must talk and respond to the content of the debate not from a written script nor from memory! You will not be persuasive if you are rolling your eyes and perspiring because you can't remember what you want to say. If you do freeze and have to refer to your notes, then try to deliver the words — don't read. Use plenty of eye contact to do this and slow down.

- <u>Do use notes</u>: to remind you what to say, to remind you when to say it, to remind you how to say it!

7. How to use **notes**

- Notes are to remind the speaker of what they want to say, that is, the main points. Therefore, your cards should have only the headings not a full script.

- They also remind the speaker of the structure of the speech, that is, the order of making the points.

- They remind the speaker of the style, that is, when to use a soft calm voice, when to be more aggressive, when to slow down.

- Have a page with the main points prioritized and numbered and any style reminders. Leave room to renumber the order if necessary — remember you need to be flexible in a debate so that you can respond to what has been said.

- Have the evidence for each main point written in note form on small thin cards — not paper — which you can hold in your hand whilst speaking on that point. Use bullet points not full text.

- Practice moving cards from front to back in your hand.

- Have spare cards to write rebuttal notes.

- If you have difficulty pronouncing certain words or remembering particular vocabulary — write words in big letters and phonetically on a spare sheet so you can see them clearly when you need them.

Vocal Aspects of Manner

1. **Volume** — don't shout but be heard

   - A loud strident harangue is as bad and off-putting as soft wishy-washy language.

- Adjust your volume to the size of the room.

- Curtains, carpets, people all absorb sound so raise your voice in this situation.

- Make important points with a slow deliberate quiet manner.

- Use the microphone. Practise — find the range — don't fiddle — if it screeches, stop talking until it settles down or has been tamed!

2. **Voice** — vary the pace and pitch of your voice

- For example, use a louder and more aggressive voice for what you may consider to be appalling statements made by the opposition but be natural — don't overdo it; otherwise you will be funny but not convincing.

- Use calm and relaxed tones to inspire confidence in your argument.

- Emphasis comes not only from volume — a point you want to emphasise can be spoken with deep conviction by speaking slowly and firmly.

3. **Speed** — don't gabble

Speed is a contentious problem. For example, in the Philippines and All Asian Debates people often speak very quickly whereas in Europe, America, Australia the delivery is much more measured! I strongly believe that if you can't be understood, there is no point in speaking. A fast rapid fire delivery may not be understood, in which case you may as well have kept quiet!

• Write "SLOW DOWN" on every second page of your notes if you have a tendency to talk quickly.

• Use clear enunciation. Do this by opening your mouth wider than you would in normal speech. Be sure your jaw is relaxed.

• Debate is formal so words should be clear and formal.

Example:

"My cotenshi is ..." is sloppy pronunciation. Ensure that you pronounce each syllable — "My <u>con</u> <u>ten</u> <u>tion</u> is ..." and be careful not to drop the endings of words — "convic <u>tion</u>" not "convict..."

• Don't speed up if running out of time. Have your main points prepared so you can use the last minute after the bell to finish what you are saying (30secs) and to repeat the main points of your argument (30secs).

• If you have a strong accent, speak a little slower.

4. **Pauses**

Use pauses to add emphasis instead of screeching or shouting.

Example:

"*The most crucial point I can make to you is (pause) that men and women are (pause) born (pause) equal!*"

"*The amount of rubbish thrown from the windows of cars and buses is (pause) disgraceful.*"

"*Smoking (pause) will (pause) kill (pause) you!*"

5. **Language** — keep language simple

- Don't use long words unless you really understand them and — most importantly — think the audience will understand them. There is no need to show off dictionary knowledge. Simple words are often the most persuasive.

- Don't use slang, colloquialisms, informal phrases, and never swear or blaspheme. It doesn't sound good to be calling on God to help you and it may be offensive to some people to hear "Oh my God" being used flippantly.

- Don't say "I honestly believe ..." as it implies you may not be always honest. Better would be "Most intelligent people understand that..."

- Never say "Right?" at the end of statements. You are not asking to be believed, you are showing that you <u>must</u> be believed because your reasoning and evidence is so persuasive.

• Short sentences are clearer, more interesting, and have greater dramatic effect. Long sentences can become a ramble in which your message gets lost.

• Clarity of expression — keep your message simple — make your evidence clear, precise and concise. For example, "The main reason we have air pollution is because we burn too much coal."

• Don't be vague. Don't say "I think I read somewhere ..." It implies that you are not sure about the strength of your argument. Say "It was reported in the press ..."

• Use formal language, for example, "Good morning/evening/ afternoon ..."

• The chairperson (if there is one) is often addressed as "Mister/ Madam Speaker".

• Address the opposition as "the opposition / the proposition" or "the affirmative / the negative side" or "the opposing side" or "the honorable ladies / gentlemen / lady and gentleman opposite".

• Address the audience as "Ladies and Gentlemen".

• There are only a few formal expressions that are common in debates. For example, "For (all) these reasons, we beg to differ", "We beg the motion fall / stand", "I propose the motion be upheld", "I oppose the motion."

6. **Signposting**

Signposting gives an impression of organisation and logic. This is generally persuasive and therefore helpful to your case. It also helps you to return to the structure of your argument after you have been diverted by rebuttals from the opposition.

• Tell your audience where you are going and then where you have been! Indicate at beginning and end how many main points you will make or have made and what they are.

Example:

"We believe that dogs are better than cats and will provide 3 reasons to support our point of view. First, dogs are more friendly. Second, you can take a dog for a walk. Third, dogs can scare off intruders." Then in your presentation you give examples to persuade your audience of each point. For example, "We know dogs are friendlier than cats because they always come running to meet us when we come home. They seem to share our moods and even to offer sympathy when we are sad. For example, ..." Conclude by saying "We propose the motion that dogs are better than cats because they 1) are friendlier, 2) can be taken for a

walk, and 3) will scare off intruders."

- When signposting, speak slowly so judges and audience can take notes. This is of particular importance when giving the definition and your side's case line (see Part 4). If the audience doesn't catch what the debate is about, then they won't be able to follow it.

- However, don't be too tightly fixed to your structure. In debate, flexibility is essential and some sparks of passion, frustration, humour or despair in response to the opposing side's arguments help to bring the debate alive, add entertainment and are likely to help your case. These won't have been signposted, but that is ok.

- Do try to signpost when making rebuttals, especially in the reply speech.

Example:

"There are two reasons why we believe the opposition's point about X is wrong. They are Y and Z."

7. Use **repetition** to add emphasis — this also can be judged under Method

Winston Churchill's famous speech during World War Two was an extremely persuasive statement of commitment. Note the repetition of "we shall fight" followed by the short dramatic phrase at the end.

> *"We shall not flag nor fail, we shall fight in France, we shall fight on the seas and oceans, we shall fight with growing confidence and growing strength in the air, we shall defend our island, whatever the cost may be, we shall fight on the beaches, we shall fight on the landing grounds, we shall fight in the fields and in the streets, we shall fight in the hills; we shall never surrender."*

Note People like Churchill and the oft quoted Martin Luther King ("I have a dream ...") had unique oratory styles which, because they were statesmen, were highly appropriate and very persuasive. However, it is important <u>not</u> to overdo this style as it can sound rather silly coming from students or people who are not — yet — statesmen.

• Repetition is a useful tool when emphasis is required.

Example:

"This policy is wrong, wrong, wrong."

Example:

"Rubbish in the streets, rubbish in the rivers, rubbish hanging in trees, rubbish, rubbish — <u>rubbish</u>! Why do we pollute our environment with rubbish?"

• Repeat important points, especially those that you think judges and audience may be writing down, for example: definitions, case lines, main arguments. Recapping important points is a valuable technique that helps to convince.

Example:

"Just so that we are clear, I repeat, we limit our use of the death penalty to 3 categories: contract killers of policemen, the leaders of the international drug trade and war criminals."

• Repeating a point by using different words is a subtle and frequently used way of being persuasive. Especially where a point is not absolutely clear first time, it is good to say it again in other words. Teachers and parents do this all the time.

Example:

"We believe that smoking should be banned because it damages hearts and lungs. It is the major cause of heart failure and it affects our ability to breathe."

8. **Humour** — a very useful tool in helping to get the audience on your side

• Debates are often won by audience reaction since even the most analytical judges will "feel" a good point has been made if the audience laughs or responds in some way.

- Debate has an element of entertainment about it — but don't overdo it. People who get carried away making jokes may lose on substance.

- Prepared jokes may fall flat if they are not made appropriately. Humour is best when it is spontaneous, relevant and in response to something said by the opposing side.

- Don't ever make personal attacks even in fun. Attack the opposing argument not the person.

- A tone of friendly rivalry is appropriate. You are friends with the opposing team, together exploring an issue but doing your best to persuade the other side to your argument; you are not enemies caught in a battle to the death.

CONCLUSION

 Manner should be sincere and respectful.

 Use clear and simple language and appropriate humour to deliver a logical, lucid and coherent argument.

 Manner must convince.

PART 4

Method

Whereas manner is how you deliver your speech, method is the strategy used to win the debate.

Method: how to do it

To be persuasive, it is generally necessary to think of a strategy rather than just firing off a series of facts and figures. This is what is being considered under the method area of judgement. Frequently the number of marks available for method is half that available for manner and matter, but that does not mean that method is unimportant. On the contrary, a loss of one mark for method may equate to two marks for manner and matter. Therefore, it is worth thinking about.

Debate strategy includes the quality of the definition, fulfilling the tasks assigned to each speaker's role, effective teamwork, clear structuring of speeches and effective use of time.

Quality of the Definition

The affirmative side has what is called its "burden". That is the duty to establish a debatable case for the motion.

1. It is necessary that all the debaters agree on what is being debated and that what is being debated is understood by the audience. It is pointless if each side is debating a different interpretation of the motion. At best, it becomes a definitional debate which is usually boring and non-productive. Definitional debates should be avoided wherever possible. (see Part 5)

2. It is necessary in parliamentary debating that the motion is interpreted in a way that there is a case to answer. In other words, the affirmative side must interpret the motion in a way that allows the opposition to challenge them. If the definition forms a truism, tautology or is unreasonably time or place set, then it does not allow the opposition to challenge and there can be no debate.

Example:

"Murder is indefensible."

This would be impossible to argue against.

Example:

A debate on education methods must not be set in Mexico in the 1920s because it is unreasonable to expect the opposition to know anything about education in Mexico let alone during the 1920s.

If the positive side has met its burden by providing a sound basis on which a debate can be held, then the negative side should have a clear case with which to debate.

The negative side should try to accept the definition proposed by the affirmative side wherever possible. (see Part 5)

The Clash

The opposition must challenge by directly confronting the affirmative side's case. They do not, however, have to stick to the exact conditions of the case as laid out by the affirmative. They can extend or narrow a topic if it helps them but must give clear reasons for doing so.

If the negative side does not challenge the affirmative side's case, they will lose on Matter as well as Method.

Allocation of Tasks

Each speaker has a role and specific function within the team and in the debate.

First Affirmative — the first speaker on the affirmative or proposing

side

1. Introduce the motion. Generally it is helpful to state — quickly —

    why the affirmative side believes the motion is important and

    of interest. This is often done by relating it to something that is

    in the news or a situation that currently or frequently affects us.

Example:

"*This House would further restrict free speech.*"

An introduction to this motion may mention, for example, a recent

violent argument between people of different races or a case of

domestic verbal abuse between husband and wife reported in the

newspapers.

2. Provide an explicit definition. This means that any ambiguous

    words in the motion must be defined and the motion narrowed

    to specifics that can be debated in the time allowed.

Example:

By "free speech" we mean currently legal phrases that are abusive

or disparaging of particular groups based on their religion, gender or ethnicity.

3. Justify the case. This is a statement — the case statement — which clearly gives the side's interpretation of the motion. It should be one sentence which indicates what the affirmative side wants to prove during the debate. It should be referred to frequently during the debate and must not change once stated.

Example:

"We believe that senior schools and universities should adopt a 'hate speech code' prohibiting speech that abuses groups on the basis of their religion, gender or ethnicity."

Note The debate has been narrowed to schools and universities and free speech narrowed to abusive language aimed at 3 specific groups of people. This is now the subject of the debate. The first affirmative speaker should not waste time discussing alternative approaches.

4. Outline the side's case. The first affirmative speaker then indicates the main points of the team's arguments and shows how their side's argument will develop and what the team is setting out to achieve.

Example:

A hate speech code is necessary because young people can be unknowingly insensitive. Hurtful remarks can have long term effects. A sense of inequality among people leads to serious and dangerous behaviour which can affect us all.

5. Present evidence. The first speaker must give some substantive argument. That is, he/she will provide some evidence to support the main points, or some of the main points, indicated.

Example:

Young people are inexperienced and may not understand the damage they can do by not recognizing all people as equals and being intolerant of differences. A young woman who is called names and cruelly teased for wearing a head scarf on religious grounds may harbour a resentment that undermines her confidence all her life — or which explodes later in some violent act of retaliation. Young people need guidance and a "hate speech code" taught and implemented in schools and universities would provide this.

First Negative — the first speaker on the negative or opposing side

1. Evaluate the given definition. An admission that the problem

underlying the case provided by the proposition is valid sets the scene for a good debate.

Example:

"Abusive language directed at anyone has no place in a civilized society. We agree that young people can be insensitive, though they can also show great sensitivity and that abusive language should have no place in schools, universities or anywhere else for that matter."

2. Accept or reject the definition.

Example:

"We accept the definition as provided."

Example:

"We dispute the definition provided because we feel that the 3 groups identified by the proposition are too limiting. What about verbal abuse of children by parents, abusive language used in the workplace, abuse of the elderly? A code covering religion, gender and ethnicity implies that other forms of abuse are acceptable. This is not the world we want."

If rejecting the definition the opposition must give justification and a clear alternative. (see Part 5 for more on definition) However, unless the definition provided by the affirmative side is really unreasonable, the "even if" (see Part 5) option is the best strategy to adopt since in competition, the judges, or in general, the audience, may not agree with the negative's rejection and alternative interpretation and may think the affirmative's definition reasonable. Such a situation will be bad for the negative's case.

3. Examine the case given by the affirmative side — point out flaws and refute the specific points given by the first affirmative.

Example:

"Not all young people are insensitive. Indeed many teenagers are very sensitive to situations and feelings. Forming lasting friendships is important to them so they are not generally abusive and when they are, their friends and parents are able to set them right. The opposition mentions religion, gender and ethnicity but there are many other fields of difference between people."

4. Present case for the negative side. This means providing a team case statement that refutes that of the opposition and indicates what the negative team will set out to achieve. The first negative must set up the clash — the challenge to the

affirmative's case.

Example:

"We do <u>not</u> believe that senior schools and universities should adopt a 'hate speech code' prohibiting speech that abuses groups on the basis of their religion, gender or ethnicity. We believe that to do so will not prevent the use of abusive language in wider contexts, that a hate speech code will be impossible to implement and that to further restrict free speech is against our interests. We oppose the motion."

Second Affirmative — the second speaker on the affirmative side

1. Deal with the definition <u>if</u> it is still an issue. If the definition has been accepted, there is no need to mention it. If it has been disputed, the second affirmative should address any issues.

Example:

"We have limited our definition to religious, gender and ethnic abuse because these are the three areas in which abuse is most frequent, can do the most damage and in which the law does not currently have specific influence."

2. Refute the opposing side's case and their supporting material.

It is best to attack the substance rather than the example unless the example is clearly irrelevant.

3. Deepen and extend the affirmative side's substantive argument.

Second Negative — the second speaker on the negative side

1. Refute the affirmative's case.

2. Deepen and extend the negative side's substantive argument.

Third Negative — the third speech for the negative side, given usually by the first speaker where there are only two speakers

1. Compare and contrast the two cases. Address the main issues.

2. Highlight weaknesses in the affirmative case. This is the main role and should be given the most time.

3. Emphasise the strengths in the negative side's argument.

4. Reiterate the negative side's case statement.

Third Affirmative — the third speech for the affirmative side, given usually by the first speaker where there are only two speakers

1. Rebut the negative side's case.

2. Summarise affirmative side's case.

3. Compare and contrast the arguments.

4. Reiterate the affirmative side's case statement.

> The third speech is sometimes called the **reply speech** or summary speech. Where there are only two members of each team, the reply speech is usually given by the first speaker of each team.
>
> • The negative side speaks first.
>
> • No new information or argument can be given during a reply speech since there will be no opportunity for it to be properly refuted and answered.
>
> • Speakers should address the decisive issues that have been highlighted by the debate. They should not waste time on unimportant details.
>
> • The reply speech should summarise the main points and show how the important arguments of the opposing side have been undermined and how the side's arguments have been shown to be stronger.

Teamwork

• Work together — help each other.

• Don't "steal" each other's material. The first speaker should lay out the argument with some evidence. The second speaker should deepen the argument with more evidence: facts, figures, examples, reasoning.

• The most important points should be made early in the debate so that they can be addressed and answered. They must not be left to the third speech.

• Support your teammate.

Example:

> *Don't say "the point my teammate was trying to make was...", say "Let me expand on the point my teammate made so well and which the opposition seems to have failed to grasp."*

• Pass notes where possible.

• Make rebuttals as early as possible — don't leave them for your teammate or a later speech.

• Allocate tasks — such as the writing down of the opposition's definition and main points.

• Don't add new arguments after the first bell — finish your point and move on to your summary. Aim to leave a strong impression not a flurried exit.

Speech Structure

• Be organised and well prepared.

• Have enough relevant material. It is best to have more than you think you can use — you don't know what the opposition might throw at you.

• Structure your speech so you know which points you have covered — be able to summarise what you have said.

• Be flexible to the dynamics of the debate. You are not debating if you merely state your argument without reference to the opposition's argument. The most effective method is to be able to integrate your rebuttals of the opposing argument with your own points.

Example:

The opposition argues that each person has the right to determine what is or is not bad but we contend that smoking damages health and that this puts an unreasonable burden on the health service and therefore on society. This is not and should not be an individual choice because it adversely affects society.

• Develop the points adequately. In a debate on terrorism, don't just say "Look at South Africa for example." Give the details of the example and say <u>how</u> it relates to your point.

Example:

"South Africa is a good example of my point that liberation groups

who renounce violence are more likely to succeed. For instance, apartheid was only ended in SA after the ANC renounced violence. This goes to our case that terrorism often alienates the very groups from which support is needed and so peaceful means are more effective."

Note Developing points adequately is extremely important when using the English language. It is up to the speaker (or writer) to make themselves crystal clear. It is not for the listener (or reader) to be able to interpret in whichever way they like.

• Prepare strong opening and closing speeches — practice and time them so you can't be caught out with timing. Be able to state the main points of your argument concisely in 30 seconds.

• Avoid superlatives, rhetorical questions and exaggerated claims.

Example:

"This policy will definitely solve all the problems of the world."

"This is the correct thing to do."

"You agree with me, right?"

"Don't you think so?"

"The famous Huangshan Mountain is known by everyone in the world."

• If you use a quotation or anecdote, refer to it again in your speech: show its relevance to your argument.

• Use statistics and expert opinion where possible. Give the source of the data.

• The third speaker must not produce any new arguments since it will be impossible for the opposition to challenge them.

• Ensure that the powerful ending to your speech summarises your main arguments and clearly states your case.

Time Management

• Make good use of time. Try to finish on the second bell not between the bells. The first bell is just there to warn you it is time to start summing up.

• Don't waste time explaining the structure of your speech in detail or telling the audience about your role — get on with the debate!

• Don't spend a long time on insignificant points or tell long rambling stories — especially about "friends" who are unknown to the audience. Any anecdotes should be short and relevant.

• Don't waste time talking about possible alternative definitions once the definition has been agreed.

CONCLUSION

 Method requires organisation.

 Individual debaters must fulfill their roles.

Teams must organise their material effectively so as to be persuasive and to be able to attack the opposing arguments.

 Issues must be critically analysed.

Arguments must be clearly structured.

Time must be well spent.

PART 5

Matter

Having talked about the manner — how you will speak and the method — the organisation of your team's case, we turn to the matter — the content of your case, your argument.

Matter: what you say

If you say nothing there is no matter; if you gibber (talk rapidly and unintelligibly) there is no matter; if you harangue the audience about something totally unrelated to the motion there is no matter. Anything you say relating to the motion is matter — it includes substantive material, that is, arguments and reasoning, examples, case studies and facts; refutation (rebuttal); points of information and, of course, the definition.

The Definition

A good definition clarifies the motion by highlighting the issue that the motion is addressing and focusing it to specific arguments. It ensures that the issues are clear to both sides and to the audience.

- Sides <u>have to debate the same issue</u>; otherwise the debate will become a game of tennis or ping-pong with no progression or conclusion. Debates about the definition and debates where examples pass back and forth with no interaction are boring and tedious because no progress is made and no conclusion reached. The best debates are arguments over substantial points, that is, over the reasoning for the arguments.

• The definition must be linked and <u>clearly relevant to the motion</u>.

• The definition <u>must be debatable</u>, that is, it must have at least two sides to it.

• It is necessary to know what is being debated; otherwise it is impossible to know who has won. <u>So it is necessary for the teams to agree the terms of the debate</u>.

• The definition provides the scope (boundaries) of what will be in the debate and what is not relevant. It narrows or broadens the motion and clarifies the terms.

• The definition <u>must not seek to confuse or derail</u> the opposition. If there are clearly other interpretations of a motion, it is necessary for the first affirmative speaker to quickly justify the choice of definition. Their decision should be based on what is topical and what would appeal to the audience.

Example:

"We should clean up our act." This could be a corruption debate or an environmental debate. Interpreted as an environmental debate, for example, the first affirmative might say: "With the Olympics coming in 2008, Beijing is keen to show its best face to the world. Therefore we all have responsibility to clean up our act. Our case is that this can not be left only to the municipal government because all individuals have a moral and civic responsibility to keep their environment clean wherever they live." The issue of this debate is the line between individual responsibility and government responsibility with regard to the environment. The arguments for and against will explore where this "line" can be drawn.

- The definition once agreed <u>must not be changed</u>, so be sure everyone in the team agrees the definition — second or third speakers must not redefine the motion.
- The <u>negative side must accept or reject the definition</u> offered by the affirmative. (see The Negative Side's Definition and Rejecting the Definition)

Defining the Motion

1. Isolate the issue — define the subject

Example:

"This house believes a carrot is better than a stick." Do not define carrot and stick — that would be silly! <u>Think about the issue</u> — incentive and reward versus fear and punishment as a method of motivation.

Example:

"This house would swim against the tide." The issue here is to do with conformity. The affirmative may define the motion in general terms: for example, that it is better not to conform. Or they may choose to narrow the motion and choose a topical issue.

2. Set the scope. Having isolated the issue, define the subject by setting the scope.

Example:

Who and where is the motion relevant to — all people, Chinese, students ...?

Example:

If "school" is in the motion, define what type of school: primary, middle, high, private, public, training, dog schools.

Example:

"This house believes a carrot is better than a stick."

The debate could be about methods of motivation in education (schools), parenting, law and order or the workplace.

3. Define ambiguous words in the motion or in your definition that may lead to confusion. Do not define every word nor known terms such as *abortion* or *euthanasia*.

   • Define words by using commonly accepted definitions. Try to keep away from dictionary definitions and certainly don't get into a "my dictionary is better than yours" argument. Don't list all the possible meanings of the word — just say which meaning you will use.

Example:

We define "the market" in the general sense of the global market in which trade and commercial activity takes place competitively.

Example:

By "punishment" we mean any form of physical punishment which causes physical pain or injury.

Example:

Welfare could mean: food stamps, farm subsidies, education, healthcare, pensions or unemployment benefits. Reform could mean: change (if so, how), abolish, reduce or expand.

Therefore, an example of a definition of welfare reform could be: "By 'welfare reform', we mean specific changes to healthcare. The changes we propose are 1) free consultations with a qualified doctor for everyone over 60 or in full-time education and 2) a standard charge of no more than 5 yuan for all medicines prescribed by a doctor."

• Terms in common usage must be used that way and not redefined to confuse the opposition.

Example:

"The Greens" are widely known to be environmentalists, not Martians from outer space.

• Any comparative expressions, such as "bigger, better, smaller" or expressions such as "we should" may require an explanation of how they can be evaluated.

Example:

Does "we" refer to us here in this room, in China, in the world? How should we do it — through legislation, a nationwide public awareness campaign or individually?

Example:

"This policy will make people's lives better by increasing disposable

incomes in the agricultural sector by 20%." The reasoning will have to include statistics to support this figure.

4. There are no rules about expanding or narrowing the definition, but it is generally better to go into detail rather than to look at generalizations that can be difficult to prove and for which there may be many exceptions.

The Negative Side's Definition

It is tempting for the negative side to produce their own definition, that is, their interpretation of the motion. (This is sometimes allowed in the early stages of teaching debate.) However, both sides giving their own interpretation and definition will generally lead to a debate about definitions which will not progress the argument nor produce an effective conclusion. Remember that the purpose of formal debate is to test a policy or theory promoted by the affirmative side. Assuming manner and method skills are the same on both sides, the negative side can usually only win if they show that the affirmative side's arguments are insufficiently strong.

To overcome the temptation to start a definitional debate, the negative side should consider the possible issues addressed by the motion rather than preparing for one particular issue. They are then in a better position to take on the definition given by the affirmative side.

The negative side must relate their case to the agreed definition, <u>not</u> to their preferred definition. However, if they consider the affirmative side's definition to be flawed, they can use the even-if argument. They may also proffer their definition but must continue to debate the affirmative side's definition. The affirmative side may choose to rebut the negative side's definition and then both definitions may be debated in parallel.

The **even-if** argument works on the principle — "We consider your interpretation inaccurate but agree to debate it on the premise that even if you are right in your definition we still oppose you and your argument."

Example:

> *"Even though we think your definition too narrow, we will debate it as you ask since we still disagree with you."*

Note Although both sides have to attempt to prove their case, the negative side does not have to provide an alternative to the affirmative side's case. They only have to disprove it.

Example:

> *"This House would ban corporal punishment in schools."*

The negative side has only to disprove the policy as being unreasonable or ineffective. It does not have to provide alternative punishments and prove they work.

Rejecting the Definition

If rejecting, the negative side must say why. That is, they must justify their decision and offer an alternative definition. They should only reject a definition on grounds that it is unreasonable or unarguable. Be aware that the judges and audience may not agree it is unreasonable.

Example:

The motion, "This House would not smoke" defined in terms of the issue about drug abuse is acceptable. However, if the affirmative side's case is that the motion should stand because drug abuse increases the spread of Aids and that drunkenness leads to violence, the negative side can reasonably object since injecting drugs and drinking alcohol has nothing to do with smoking.

In this case the negative side could say, "We consider the definition unreasonable because injecting, eating or drinking narcotics or stimulants has nothing to do with the motion that expressly mentions smoking. However, we do consider that smoking both legal tobacco and illegal drugs such as cocaine should be banned because they injure health and are antisocial."

In the example above, the negative side has then accepted the issue promoted by the affirmative but have properly linked the definition and their case to the motion.

The Case Statement

Having provided a definition, the affirmative side must then state clearly in one sentence their position. This should be an all-encompassing reason for the team's position which serves as a prop for all other arguments. Teams must provide a clear statement of <u>why</u> they are adopting their stance. This is called the case statement, case line or team line.

The case statement is a general statement of the reason for the team's position on the motion. It acts like a topic sentence in a well written paragraph. It provides the basis for all the points raised by the side. This is why it is sometimes called the team line.

The first speaker on the negative side, having agreed the definition, will also give their case statement by negating what the affirmative side has said and sometimes expanding or restricting the affirmative side's position.

The negative side may also give their own definition's case statement where they think the affirmative's definition is flawed. It may then be that both definitions will be debated under the 'even-if' form.

The case statement answers the question "Why is it generally true/ untrue to say that ..."

Example:

Smoking should be banned in public places because it harms health, pollutes the atmosphere and adversely affects non-smokers.

Smoking should not be banned in public places because to do so would be an infringement of civil rights. (These rights are more important than the small amount of damage done to health and the atmosphere.)

The case statement is very important. It will help ensure that you debate the motion and don't go off at a tangent.

Example:

"This House believes that there is too much violence on TV" should not be debated as if it were already the case by explaining why there is too much violence (because people like watching violence, perhaps). An acceptable case statement would be "There is too much violence on TV because the violence on TV is creating a more

violent society."

This prevents debaters from missing the point of the debate and thinking what they are trying to prove, for example in the motion above, <u>why</u> there is too much violence rather than <u>whether</u> there is too much violence on TV. The motion and definition form a hypothesis that has to be discussed in the debate. The motion is <u>not</u> a proven statement.

Example:

"This house would swim against the tide."

A suitable case statement would be "We believe that individualism is best because it allows for greater innovation and progress."

Or, if the motion has been narrowed: a case statement could be "We believe that China should not conform to international trade rules in the agricultural sector because they are injurious to domestic economic growth." During the debate, the affirmative side would produce a number of points (reasons) for their position and support them with reasoning, examples, statistics, expert opinion, etc. The negative side would argue that China should obey the rules and would attempt to show how the reasoning by the affirmative side is mistaken.

The case statement provides a useful point of cohesion and clarifies the side's argument. Teams should repeat their case statement frequently throughout the debate so that the audience has a clear understanding of each side's position.

Case Preparation

Teams may have different amounts of time to prepare. In competition this is generally limited but when teaching debate or in life generally, preparation time should be as long as possible. Taking time to research topics will help to identify the various relevant issues and will provide information and statistics to support arguments.

Note Many people find it hard to argue for something with which they personally disagree. Remember it is the issue that is at stake not your personal beliefs.

Say what you know — Use the arguments — Be objective.

- Identify the background to the motion and identify and isolate the issues that the motion could be addressing.
- Decide from which issue you will produce a definition.

If you are the affirmative, then choose to define the motion in the way that has the least number of counter arguments or the weakest counter argument but which will be acceptable to a reasonable person and which is of topical interest.

If you are the negative and there is more than one possible issue, you have to prepare for as many possible cases as you can along with the counter arguments.

- Don't spend too long trying to second-guess what the opposition will say. Better to identify the issues and possible cases from both sides so you can attack the affirmative side's points. <u>In debate, it is better to attack than defend</u>!

- Be sure that all members of the affirmative team are aware of the <u>agreed definition</u>.

- <u>Analyse!</u> Look into the reasons why and examples of how that relate to the motion. Note down any facts/statistics/data.

- Whilst all arguments are matter, some are better than others.

Example:

In a debate on legalizing euthanasia, an argument that we should all have the right to determine our own destiny will be considered much stronger than an argument for legalising euthanasia in order to provide jobs for the funeral industry.

- Try not to use old matter.

Example:

The hole in the ozone layer was interesting and good matter in the 1980s — now it is old.

- Plan who will be mainly responsible for which parts of the arguments — case allocation. (see below)

- <u>Structure the argument</u> so that there is an introduction and conclusion.

- <u>Prioritise</u> the arguments so that you can apportion time effectively.

- <u>Make notes about delivery</u>, that is, make a note to pause, to slow down, to soften your voice, etc.

Case Allocation

Teams must have a consistent approach, that is, they must work together. Teams must allocate the arguments (the matter) effectively so that both members of the team have clear roles and arguments. If the first to speak says it all and leaves nothing for the second speaker, they will be marked down on method.

However, don't leave your best arguments to the second speaker — plan to get them out early in the debate so they can be shown to be strong and effective and so that the opposition has plenty of time to argue against them. You don't debate by just saying the point — you have to substantiate it. The second speaker can take the substantiation to a deeper level.

If the case statement is divided between the two speakers, then the first negative can only argue against half of the affirmative side's argument. Therefore, it is always best to <u>divide the material that proves the case statement instead of dividing the case statement</u>.

In other words, do not split the case statement by giving one speaker one part and the other the second part. This will lead to a "hung case" which shows lack of teamwork and may cause loss of the debate if one speaker's argument is destroyed.

Example:

"Love and marriage go together like a horse and carriage."

It would be a mistake for the first speaker to talk only about love and to leave the second speaker to talk about marriage. The motion is indicating that love <u>and</u> marriage are related in the same way as a horse <u>and</u> carriage. That is the subject of the debate.

Example:

"This House believes that there is too much violence on TV."

Don't allocate "a discussion of <u>how much</u> violence there is on

TV" to the first speaker and "<u>why</u> this amount of violence is

bad" to the second speaker.

Better would be for the first affirmative to say that there is too

much violence on TV because it is a factor in increasing levels of

violence in society (examples), it changes traditionally accepted

behaviour (examples) and it frightens children (examples). The

second speaker could then develop these arguments with more

examples and statistics.

Sometimes it may be useful to allocate material on social/economic grounds; past/present; local/global, etc. However, when doing this, ensure that the arguments inter-relate with each other and are firmly tied to the case statement. Generally it is best to avoid practical/ theoretical and good/bad grounds as this can lead to difficulties as to where the division lies. Better would be for the two speakers to prove the case in two distinct ways. This means more material for the opposition to deal with.

If conceding that there are some negative points in the case you are presenting but that the good outweigh the bad, make the argument clear and be sure to justify it.

Example:

"Of course giving free medical consultations to only the young and

the elderly is unfair but it is a first step towards free healthcare for all and it ensures that the poorest and most vulnerable people are given the care they need." Follow this with some specific examples.

Making the Case

- Keep thinking flexibly. Don't ignore everything else just because you come up with a brilliant idea. One idea is only part of the process of winning the overall argument — the debate!

- Quantify wherever possible. It is more difficult to argue against a known quantity than against something which is vague and qualitative since these can have many equally valid interpretations.

- Try to ensure that your chain of argument works for each link. That is, each point and reason makes sense on its own as well as as part of the larger argument.

- After proving each point with analysis and examples, refer back to the case statement — do this frequently and with each point.

- Avoid clichés, facile statements and rhetorical questions.

Example:
_____

> *"As everyone knows ..." is not persuasive.*

Example:
_____

> *"We should all do our best" is a pointless statement.*

Example:

> *"Right?" or "Don't you agree?" makes the audience want to shout*
>
> *"No!"*

Truisms and Tautologies

Be aware that truisms and tautologies are not in the spirit of debate. Your argument must be falsifiable in order to work. In other words, your proposition must be able to be rebutted.

Example:

> *"An island is land surrounded by water, so Australia is an island"*
>
> *is tautology. It would be impossible for the opposition to argue*
>
> *that Australia is not an island despite it being thought of as a*
>
> *continent.*

Example:

> *"Smoking is bad for health" is a truism. However, you could say*
>
> *"Because so many people suffer smoking related illnesses, the*
>
> *health service is under great strain. Banning smoking in public*
>
> *places would help reduce this."*

> *This could be rebutted with, "There is no proof that people*
>
> *would reduce the number of cigarettes they smoke. How often*
>
> *do you see people standing outside or crowding into designated*
>
> *smoking rooms, at airports for example?"*

Rebuttal

Sitting back listening to a good and interesting speech may be enjoyable but it isn't debating. Furthermore, in order to win a debate, it is not enough to provide a well reasoned argument for your case. Remember there are always two sides in a debate. The opposing side has to question — attack — the arguments provided and seek to show up the weaknesses. Therefore, disagreement is fundamental to debate and rebuttal is how you disagree with and undermine the opposing side's argument.

It is initially and primarily the negative side's duty to do this, so that the affirmative side will have to be prepared to defend their case. However, as the negative side will also be developing arguments in support of their own case statement (usually the opposite to that provided by the affirmative), the affirmative side will have to attack as well as defend. The negative side will therefore have to do likewise. There is, therefore, an exchange of constructive (substantive argument) and destructive (rebuttal and refutation) arguments that flows backwards and forwards throughout the debate.

What to Rebut

It is important to focus on whether arguments are reasonable and logical not on whether everyone agrees with them.

Example:

You, and you may feel everyone, may believe that education should be the right of all children. However, if the opposition makes a logical argument that it is impossible in underdeveloped countries because there are insufficient teachers or money to train teachers, then that is what you should try to refute. (Perhaps by arguing that money spent on a new palace for the ruler could be spent on teacher training.)

Rebuttal should always focus on issues that are critical to the debate rather than on minor examples. Therefore, do not leap to your feet just because someone makes a minor mistake with a date which is not the main focus of their argument.

Example:

"World War Two ended in 1945 not 1946."

This is petty (unimportant) if the point being made is that it was the military strength of the atomic bomb that brought the war to an end. It would be alright to mention the mistake in passing but not to make it a major point of rebuttal by, for example, standing to make a point of information. (see Points of Information)

However, if a mistake is made that clearly affects the logic of the argument, it should be immediately pointed out. Likewise, any mistake in reasoning must be identified and attacked immediately.

Types of Rebuttal

Rebuttal can take many forms but basically they fall into one or other of the types below.

1. **Error of fact** Facts that affect the logic of the argument must be rebutted.

Example:

"ASEAN is the best forum for improving China's economy." This could be rebutted with "China is not a member of ASEAN and therefore it can not be considered a forum for China's economic development".

Example:

"The Gulf War secured Reagan's victory in 1984 and this therefore shows that people vote for leaders who win wars." This can be rebutted with "As the Gulf War didn't occur until 1991 it couldn't have affected Reagan's election and Bush (senior) who was President during the Gulf War was defeated by Clinton in 1992".

2. **Irrelevance** An example or argument that is not relevant to

the point being made must be rebutted.

Example:

The motion, "There is no such thing as a free lunch" may be revolving around the issue of whether there are too many government giveaways and freebies. If the opposing side argues that entertaining people to meals at government expense is immoral and outlines how expensive city restaurants are, the rebuttal should be that this fact is irrelevant. (It is not the expense of the meals that is at issue but the fact that the entertainment is too prevalent.) It would be pointless to argue that there are many cheap restaurants.

3. **Illogical argument** The opposition's conclusion doesn't flow logically from its premise.

Example:

The argument that "The death penalty should be kept because it deters violent crime" could be rebutted with "The state killing people hardly provides a good role model against violence to the community" or "The death penalty in the US hasn't prevented violent crime there."

4. **Unacceptable implications** In cases where the opposing side's logic is correct you may still be able to rebut on grounds of unacceptability.

Example:

> *If a side argues that legallising euthanasia would save costs in the health service. This can be rebutted by saying, "We have no right to kill sick people just to save money."*

5. **Little weight** An argument that fails to consider other causes for a situation must be rebutted.

Example:

> *Although you may have to agree with an argument that a violent film may have influenced a copycat murder, you can rebut by arguing that the film could not be the only influence (since otherwise there would be numerous murders), that more important issues were at work and therefore the argument has little weight.*

Example:

> *It may be that a speaker asserts that "increased immigration is the cause of increased unemployment." This can be rebutted by pointing out that evidence would need to be supplied to prove that the two increases were linked. Also, it may be that there are many causes of unemployment — which is the main cause? How do the various causes interact?*

6. **Contradictions and inconsistencies** These can be pointed out when speakers inadvertently contradict their teammate or

when later speakers make changes to the definition or case statement. This is why it is important to write these down as soon as they are made at the beginning of the debate. Record then accurately so you can challenge if the opposition speakers wander from them later in the debate.

How to Rebut

Rebuttal is done by exposing logical weaknesses, factual misrepresentations or weak reasoning. It should never be personal. That is, rebuttal should always attack the argument not the person — play the ball not the person!

Refuting examples is one way of rebutting, but as speakers gain maturity they will concentrate more on the point being made. Look for themes running through the opposition's arguments that are wrong.

Rebuttal is not just contradiction. If a speaker is implying that something is generally true because it is definitely true in his life, school, town or country — the opposition would be best to merely say that it is not true everywhere since different people, regions, nations have different traditions, cultures and ideas rather than finding other examples that contradict the original.

Example:
_____

> *In a debate about capital punishment, one side may have said, "The death sentence is legal in most American states." This can be rebutted with the remark, "Because the death sentence is legal in most American states doesn't mean it is everywhere."*

When you disagree with something said by the opposition, you must say <u>why you disagree</u>. It is not sufficient to say "you're wrong" or "the average person wouldn't agree" or "it might be true for you but not where I come from".

Example:
_____

> *"On your point that smoking kills people prematurely, I would like to point out that there are many dangerous pursuits that kill people, for example, mountaineering, skiing and swimming and that statistically more people die prematurely from domestic accidents than from any other cause."*

Example:
_____

> *"We disagree with your point that beauty is only ever in the eye of the beholder. Throughout history there have been commonly accepted 'beauties' who set a standard for the times. These, of course, change with time as people's ideas about what is beautiful change. For example, it is no longer considered beautiful, as it*

once was, to be fat or even plump."

Analyse the issues. A debate in which sides just throw examples and counter examples at each other without any logical or philosophical analyses is boring and not persuasive.

Example:

A debate on the motion "Adolescence is the best time in our lives" would not be good if one side lists all the ailments associated with old age — loss of teeth, hair, memory; aches and pains; diabetes, senile dementia whilst the other side counters with a list of ailments suffered by the young — spots, lack of self-confidence, anorexia, sporting injuries, unemployment. There needs to be more analysis rather than lists of "competing misery".

Alternatives

This is one of the most convincing ways of rebutting an argument. Pick holes in the solution offered by the opposition and then provide alternatives. This will cause the opposition to waste time trying to rebut the alternative rather than the motion. You can point this out once they have done so!

Example:

"The opposition argue that banning smoking in public places is

the only way to prevent people from suffering from passive smoking. This is clearly an infringement of the human and civil rights of people who smoke. We believe that installing large and effective air filters in all public places would ensure that smoke is not inhaled by non-smokers."

Rebut Absolute Cases

Words like "always", "never" can be rebutted by finding just one example that doesn't fall into the category. However, this is not usually enough of an argument to win a debate. Teams are not being asked to prove an absolute even if the motion is worded to include an absolute. If the motion does include an absolute, sides should not make the mistake of thinking that they have to prove or disprove it.

Pre-emptive Rebuttal

It is tempting, especially when there is a lack of material, for a side to suggest arguments that the opposing side may put forward. However, it is best not to do this as the opposing side can then argue that you are doing their job for them or trivializing the debate.

Example:

If a speaker says "The opposing side is likely to argue ... but we don't agree because ...", it allows the other side to say "The opposition is bringing up points for us and rebutting them itself, but these are not points that we consider important to our argument. Rather we argue that ...”

Note First negative and the second speakers should be careful not to spend all their time in rebuttal — they must remember to develop their own arguments as well. (see Part 4)

Reply Speech Rebuttal

The third speakers should adopt a compare and contrast approach to rebuttal where they try to show that the opposition's approach is inferior compared with their own side's case.

The objective is to show how one team's case is better than the other, rather than that anyone has spoken the "absolute truth". Most of the reply speech should be given to this with only perhaps 25% of the time given to reiterating the main arguments and case statement of their side.

Points of Information

Rebuttal, generally, should be done as soon as possible after a point has been made because the point will stand and may become fixed in people's minds until it has been knocked down. Therefore, it is best to interrupt as soon as the opposition has made a point with which you can disagree. To do this you must ask for a point of information (POI).

A point of information is a short comment or question relating to what is currently being said. It can not be about something said in a previous speech or earlier in the present speech unless it is to point out a contradiction to what is being currently said.

Rules pertain as to the timing of POIs. Generally speakers must not be interrupted by a POI during the first and last minute of their speech and POIs are not allowed during reply speeches.

Giving a point of information shows that you are listening and are engaged in the debate. It also shows you are confident in your argument.

How to Give a Point of Information

To give a POI, stand up, put your right hand on your head and extend the other arm towards the speaker and say "On a point of information, Sir/Madam" or "Point Sir/Madam!"

• You are more likely to be accepted if you wait for a pause. A speaker is not likely to accept your point if he is in full flow on an important point of his argument.

- It is best to let weak points go and attack the stronger points in the opposing argument.

- Some speakers like to harangue the opposing speaker with many points —this can be off-putting for the speaker and may also annoy the judges — so be careful!

- If your POI is accepted, keep it short. This is <u>not</u> an opportunity for making a speech. You should make your point in no more than 10-15 seconds.

Accepting POIs

Accepting POI shows that you are confident in your argument and ready to face challenge. This is a vital part of debate.

- When you accept a point, deal with it immediately. Don't let the person offering the point go on too long. Once you have grasped what they are saying, cut in and reply as succinctly as possible.

- Never let a POI stand without a response.

- Never agree with a POI unless it actually backs up your argument. Sometimes, the opposing speaker makes a mistake or words his point in such a way that you can turn it to your advantage.

- Always dismiss POIs as irrelevant or incorrect — but remember to say why! If you can not give a good reason why the point is unimportant then it may stand.

After the debate is concluded and the judges have delivered their verdict, it is normal courtesy for the winning side to cross the floor of the house and shake hands with the losing side!

CONCLUSION

Matter requires:

 A sensible definition that addresses the motion.

 A clear case statement that identifies your team's position in relation to the motion.

 Sufficient effective arguments with clear reasoning that support that position.

 Refutation of opposing arguments wherever possible.

PART 6

Judgement

It is a great honour to be asked to judge a debate but also a great responsibility. People who take part in public debates will have spent an enormous amount of time preparing and are extremely brave to stand up in public and espouse their views. Speakers should be accorded proper respect. Therefore, it is very important that judges are equally well prepared and take great care when making comments. A careless remark can do untold damage to developing confidence. On the other hand, ineffective comments that provide no feedback fail to help and appear derogatory.

Guidelines for New Judges

• A debate is not a collection of speeches so do not just assess language skills. So long as the language can be understood, it is not very important if the grammar or pronunciation is not perfect.

• Criteria vary so the criteria relevant for each competition must be clear in judges' minds beforehand.

• The information given previously under the 3 categories: Manner, Method, Matter should be clearly understood by any judge.

• Judgement must be fair. Bias of any kind or for any reason is unacceptable.

• Judges must bring an open mind to the proceedings. They must not expect speakers to follow any preconceived argument, to have expert knowledge nor to say what the judge thinks they should say. Speakers are not mind readers and are, in any case, entitled to their own point of view.

• Wherever possible, there should be a panel of judges — at least three. This helps to off-set the problem of subjectivity, such as what is "reasonable".

• Judges are responsible for ensuring all rules and criteria are complied with and fairly implemented.

Adjudication Notes

It is impossible to evaluate any debate by just listening. It is necessary to take notes of the arguments — even if you have heard them many times before. This is because it is how a team uses the arguments that matters most, not whether they are able to identify all known arguments nor whether the arguments they use are the most profound. Of course, a team may suddenly surprise by coming up with a new or unusual angle and this must be noted and assessed as to whether it is properly relevant.

All arguments should be noted for two other reasons:

1. Has a point been clearly substantiated? Beware of speakers who assert with a brilliant manner but fail to convince on logic or reason.

2. Has the opposing side been able to rebut them and how well did they do this? Rebuttal may be done immediately, but may also be done later in the debate. As arguments fly back and forth, it is necessary to keep track of how they are being used and whether they can stand as having been persuasive.

This is usually done by dividing your paper into columns for each speech and noting the main arguments and reasoning as it occurs. Leave plenty of space between your notes so that POIs and rebuttals can also be noted.

Notes and marks about individual speakers should be made during the debate so that it is not just the final speeches that have the greatest effect on the judges' minds and therefore on their decisions.

Judgement

Any good judge should be able to justify their decision based on the criteria. This is what is usually going on when judges retire to consider their decisions.

Judges have to decide:

- Who has won the debate and why.

- What is the margin between the teams and why.

- What mark to award each team and why.

- What mark to award each speaker and why.

Judges should assess whether the manner used was effective and reasonable. They should not expect all speakers to have the same manner. Personal style is good in debate. It is whether it is effective, persuasive and reasonable that should be assessed.

Judges should assess the strategy and teamwork displayed. Definition, for example, can be considered under method as whether the first affirmative met their burden by providing a sensible definition and whether the negative side responded appropriately.

Matter must be persuasive and credible. The definition can also be assessed here in terms of the quality of the interpretation of the motion. On the other hand, exaggerated claims, inappropriate language, assertions without substantiation, illogical assumptions or lack of rebuttals should be marked down.

Grading

There are different ways of grading. For the World University Debating

Competition rules, see http://www.britishdebate.com/resources/ judgewudcrules.asp.

Timing

Judges must ensure proper timing is kept and arrange for speakers to have warning when their time is nearly up and when it is up. This is usually done by a bell being rung or a gavel struck one minute before the end and at the end of the allotted time.

Evaluation

It is normal after all competitive debates that one of the judges gives an evaluation of the debate. In this they indicate why the winning team won and what were the strengths and weaknesses of each team and each speaker.

The experience of the various speakers must be considered and it must be remembered that the purpose of evaluation is to help and to justify the judges' decision. Therefore, if any weaknesses are mentioned, advice should be given as to how they may be overcome. The evaluation must highlight the reasons for the result.

Caveat to All Debaters

Even with the provision of clear criteria, there is a degree of subjectivity in the judgement of debate. There is no possibility that strictly adhering to a simple list of criteria will lead to certain success. What it will have led to is greater understanding, increased knowledge, food for thought and, hopefully, new friendships.

References

■ Auckland Debating Association. See www.ada.org.nz; acc. 16/09/2004.

■ Constitution of the Ninth FLTRP Cup National English Debating Competition (unpublished). Beijing, 2005.

■ D'Cruz R, ed. Australia-Asia Debating Handbook (unpublished).

■ English Online. It Comes as a Great Surprise: Speechmaking, Language Features. See http://english.unitecnology.ac.nz/resources

■ Fetterol D. How to Debate. See www.st-philiphoward.w-sussex.sch.uk/pubspeak; acc. 29/09/2004.

■ Flynn C. See www.debating.net; acc. 10/10/2004.

■ Motions Commentary. See www.chekyang.com/debating/motions

■ Philips J and Hooke J. (1998) *The Sport of Debating*. Sydney: University of New South Wales Press Ltd.

■ The English Speaking Union. Resources for Judges. See www.britishdebate.com/resources; acc. 13/11/2004, 29/9/2004.

■ University of St. Andrews Union Debating Society. See www.debatingsociety.org.uk; acc. 27/10/2003.

■ World Debating Website. See www.debating.net

Index